# Testament

*The Epic Journey of Yggdrasil*

Nothing
is Absolute
Yggdrasil
All is
Permitted

# Testament

## The Epic Journey of Yggdrasil

### Kask

Translation, Illustrations, & Design
Keith Senkowski

Foreword by
Luke Crane

How to spell and pronounce words that don't directly translate into English is always a challenge with texts like this. Originally in Old Peersha, I have attempted to translate the text by taking into consideration both accuracy and the poetic expectations of a story told aloud. This has led to only proper nouns remaining untranslated. Each of these words should be pronounced using English as a guide with the following exceptions:

| | |
|---|---|
| U | is pronounced as the *oo* in *book* |
| E | is pronounced as the *ea* in *head* |
| O | is pronounced as the *o* in *bone* |
| A | is pronounced as the *aw* in *saw* |
| I | is pronounced as the *i* in *split* |
| EE | is pronounced as the *ee* in *free* |
| Y | is pronounced as the *ya* in *yawn* |

Published by South Side Goods, Chicago, IL 60615



www.keithsenkowski.com

To Ed Kalke and Ken Orestead.

I didn't know it at the time, but you kicked me in the ass and sent me down this path. Great mentors are hard to find and I got lucky with two.

# Foreword


*You say we are the future*
*When will you ever learn?*
*A testament*
*Born out of desperation*

**Disfear, Testament,
Live the Storm, 2008**

Dear reader, you hold in your hand a most curious object. It seems a book, but if it is, it is a rare type, not often produced in our over-manufactured age. Regardless of its nature, its origin is singular. Conceived by one mind and executed painfully—every letter, every brushstroke—by a single set of hands. Like a monk at his labors in the scriptorium, the author laid upon each page each word, each wash of color, with brush and pen. His was a desperate and futile prayer to contain the gods and demons within.

Permit me to point to the most obvious detail regarding what you hold in hand: Its creator has seen fit to title it *testament*. Obvious yet significant, the word repeats on the frontispiece, a gorgeous painted block print of a lectern piled with book, quill and candle. The scrollwork contains the unequivocal bold lettering: TESTAMENT. And the word recurs again in the first sentence of the work as an attestation by the book's titular narrator, Kask: *. . . this is my testament.* And thus we ritualistically intone the word thrice to signal that, by taking up the book, opening its covers and reading its first sentence we, the readers, enter a new world. The world in which this testament was born out of desperation.

The choice to dub this collection *Testament* is no superficial flourish. It is the first and perhaps most direct clue pertaining to the mystery contained within. Certainly, to call this tale a testament in the literal sense is accurate. Kask, our narrator, feels he must unburden his soul before a panel of unnamed, unknowable, immortal judges. Thus he testifies in a most real way. But beyond its mundane use, the idea of the testament calls to mind the two segments, Old and New, of one of the most influential mythologies in human history. Conscious or not, that association can be no accident.

But this work is no Christian allegory, no *Pilgrim's Progress.* To your humble writer of this foreword, the most Christian-like aspect of the book seems to be that it is a revelation. It was not written, created or constructed by its author in the traditional sense, rather it was revealed to him by some power or deity, just as the terrible querubim visited awful knowledge upon Saul on his doomed road to Damascus.

> *I want you to know, brothers and sisters, that the gospel I preached is not of human origin. I did not receive it from any man, nor was I taught it; rather, I received it by revelation…"*
>
> Galatians 1:11–12, NIV[11]

Rather than cursing him to preach as Saul was, whatever unhuman power that visited the author has infected him with a disease of the mind that commands him to disgorge onto the page in word and image all that was revealed, regardless of whether or not our minds (or his) are prepared for it.

Before we continue and you find me raving, I must explain that in order to join you at the beginning of this work, dear reader, I had to submit myself to the trials hidden within and, through them, gain wisdom enough so that I might act as your guide, your lantern bearer, as you enter the strangely illumined chamber beyond. So I say with confidence that what lays before you, dear reader, is neither simple testimony, story, narrative, tale, nor saga. Contained in the form of this sumptuously illuminated tome, the author manifests no less than a mythology.

> *The first function of a mythology is to reconcile waking consciousness to the mysterium tremendum et fascinans of this universe as it is: The second being to render an interpretive image of the same, as known to contemporary consciousness.*

Campbell, Creative Mythology,
Ancient Vine, page 4

As Kask attempts to communicate his experiences, the author frenetically translates the narrator's inscrutable thoughts, cryptic words and garish imagery of these dire events for our unprepared collective consciousness. That said, as you explore it, you will find that this testament contains what Campbell refers to as a "profound respect for the inherited forms" of the myths that precede it, drawing the reader through a veil of familiarity. Within you will encounter shades of heroes from the Sagas to the Silmarillion, comforting and alien all at once. Yet this Campbellian respect is a ruse, a cleverly sculpted clay pot that the author fills with wonder and horror and then smashes to shards before the reader's eyes.

Beneath the cloak of its mysteries a mythology must have gods, heroes, and monsters. *Testament* has them aplenty. Beings of every stripe and form strive to elevate their families, clans, and desires over all others. One theme in particular recurs throughout that I believe attests to the mytho-revelatory nature of the text. Kask recounts many cycles of uplift and downfall, and at each nadir, as if manifesting a biologic survival imperative of the doomed culture, a hero appears. This figure gathers their wits and spears, repulsing the devouring darkness at extreme cost. To my mind, these figures echo the spirit of wrecca that Professor Tolkien discusses in his translation of *Beowulf*.



JRR Tolkien's Beowulf,
commentary, page 293

Kask's Testament is replete with wrecca. Skadi, Fiolsfid, Beli, Kernobog, Sanhet—not just one outcast forced to throw lots with Death, but dynasties of them, lineages, rising and falling in bloody contest, betrayed by fickle fate, pride, and time. Much like the heroes of old that among whom, Professor Tolkien notes, Beowulf was just one of many puissant exiles to live such a doom. And we note that this mythic association cannot be accidental. Beowulf itself being such a powerful and ancient myth that it has no human author.

In *Creative Mythology*, Campbell also notes that mythologies serve another function: to undergird the *"larger, more enduring cultural body."* Not only do they speak to us of the tremendous and fascinating mystery of the eternal struggle of life and death, but they seek to bestow morals and values, teaching us compassion, generosity and justice among many other virtues.

Amongst the blood-drenched wars and doom-spells recounted in Kask's ravings, we hear the strain of the familiar. The narrator speaks again and again of a people struggling to create justice, to define evil and sustain compassion. In the tempestuous struggles of the God-Queen Beli, we hear faintly the author's own voice straining amongst the unhuman chorus for which he is the medium. For this mythology reflects the powers and uncertainties of the author's own time, his fears and his angers. And no less a being than the great saint of fantasy fiction, Ursula K. LeGuin reminds us that this is no accident. In fact, such expressions of our world are inextricably bound into our fantastical creations:

> *The politics were there all along— the hidden politics of the hero-tale, the spell you don't know you're living under till you cast it off. . . . the world apart of a fantasy inevitably refers back to this world. All the moral weight of it is real weight. The politics of fairyland are ours.*
>
> **Ursula K. LeGuin,**
> **Revisioning History**

The tangled images and emotions of frustration, anxiety and rage conjured by the author, the recognizable icons that recall the politics of our own convulsing world, summon to our minds the rasping prophecies of Tomas Lindberg and his punk band, Disfear. Though separated from the vessel of Kask's testimony by 15 years and a massive ocean, we hear his voice chanting similar chords and polyphonies. Tormented by the same unhuman forces as the author, Lindberg creates his own Testament. And reflecting Kask's imagery, Disfear's distorted chords and driving beats ring with familiar anger, frustration, fear, and defiance.

> *We dream of poison*
> *Of annihilating liberation*
> *We are too young for mercy*
> *We are the revolution*
> *Come on!*
>
> **Disfear, Testament**
> **Live the Storm, 2008**

We could imagine Hardrik's bereaved son Eisolos shouting the very same before his oppressors.

Beyond the angst and fear, gods and heroes, beyond invention and time, I detect another, mournful strain interweaving the mad melody of both Kask's *Testament* and the author's own voice, struggling to be heard through the tumult. These chords resonate so low that one can only feel them, rather than hear them— deeper, unanswerable fears for one's children, for the destruction of the natural world through humanity's carelessness, and a creeping existential dread. For us death is a singular experience, perhaps even a mercy. When we pass on, we are reassured that our world continues and our works still live within it. But within Kask's *Testament* we feel a chthonic hum building into a scream that will not dislodge from the throat: it is the mortal fear of annihilation.

Not the mercy of death, but an atavistic horror that our struggles were never to amount to anything because darkness, time and tide shall crush us under hoof like so many ants or—even more chilling—an inchoate panic that our very own works will unleash a Hell upon creation and destroy us and everything we could ever hold dear.

In these reflections, I am reminded of another author who struggled to express this abject terror in his works. He writes:

*We live on a placid island of ignorance in the midst of black seas of infinity, and it was not meant that we should voyage far. The sciences, each straining in its own direction, have hitherto harmed us little; but some day the piecing together of dissociated knowledge will open up such terrifying vistas of reality, and of our frightful position therein, that we shall either go mad from the revelation or flee from the deadly light into the peace and safety of a new dark age.*

HP Lovecraft,
The Call of Cthulhu

Dear reader, I am confident you will find that Kask attests to Lovecraft's prophecy: He witnesses this selfsame madness and flight into ignorance, time and again. Thus I submit that this is no mere story—no biography of a single person's life—but a warning *"not of human origin"* regarding the tremendous mystery of life. A life so terrifying no fearsome band of heroes can stand against it and remain unscathed in mind or body. And so shall you find yourself friend, at the conclusion of Kask's utterances, scarred, changed utterly and fearful—but forewarned.

Luke Ansgar Crane,
Astoria, New York City, New York State, United States of America, Earth, Sol, Oort Cloud, Local Interstellar Cloud, Local Bubble,
Orion Arm, Milky Way, Local Group, Virgo Supercluster, Laniakea Supercluster, the Universe, Prime,
2/29/2024

Gishek Degom
Medyo Degom
Adan Degom
Argn Degom
Ysk
Ulfareeum
Stehreise
Heghelwos Mahr
Astras Degom
Skurmos Doru

Testament

Forever we struggle to remember
Looking for meaning, hoping to find truth

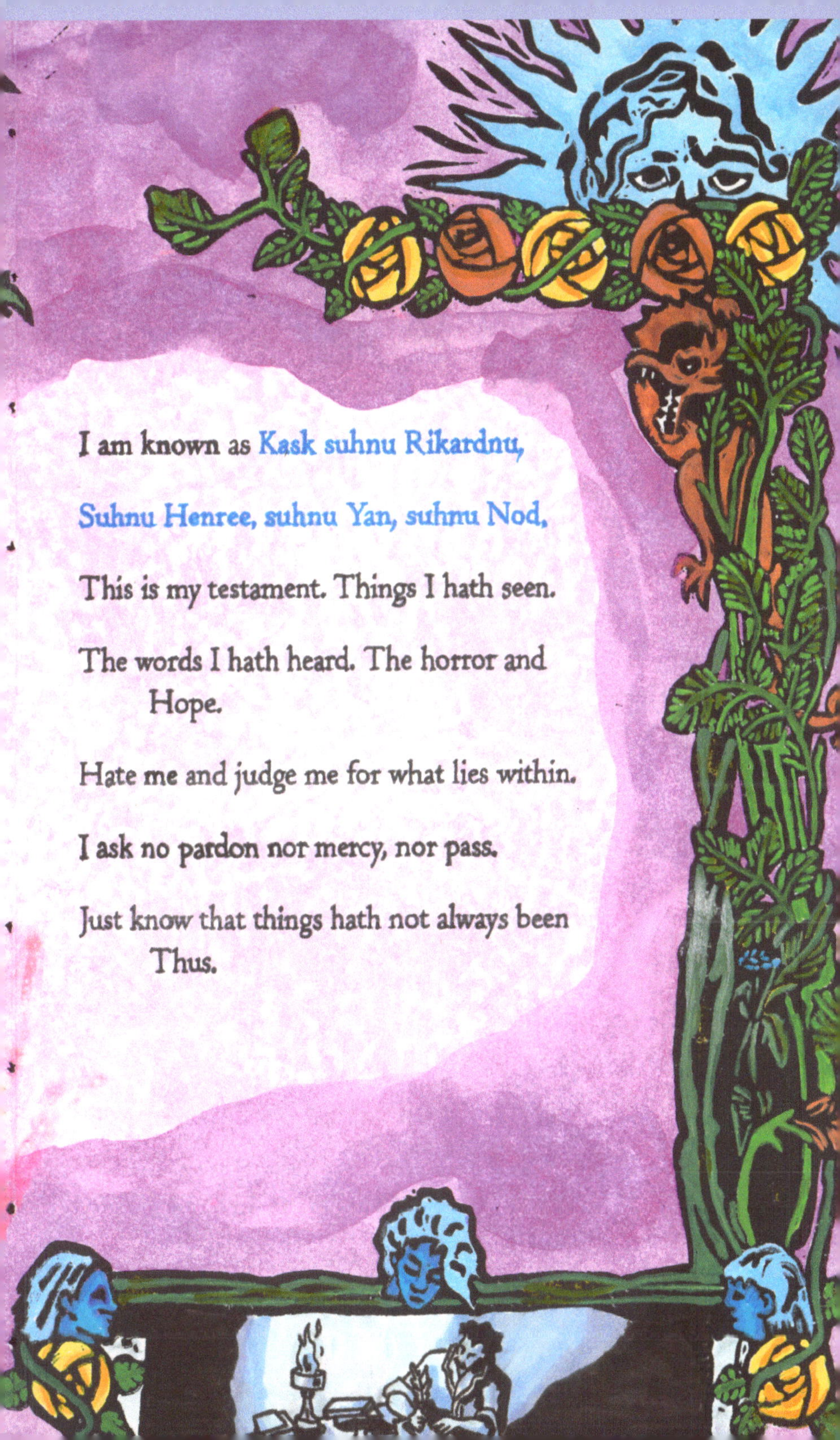

I am known as Kask suhnu Rikardnu,

Suhnu Henree, suhnu Yan, suhnu Nod,

This is my testament. Things I hath seen.

The words I hath heard. The horror and
Hope.

Hate me and judge me for what lies within.

I ask no pardon nor mercy, nor pass.

Just know that things hath not always been
Thus.

Heusos

Witness! The truth of the story within!

For there are no beginnings and no ends.

There is only dreams. Only memory.

I remember a city, fair, and bright.

Twas the city sitting upon a hill.

That shining city. That beacon of hope.

Yet fear lived without. Disorder within,

In this place did a great evil take root,

Infecting what once was full of promise.

Wealth and well wishes would not heal these
    Wounds.

From darkness the Orange Prince took Power.

The great oppressor. King of Corruption.

Bringing out the worst. The vile. The Foulest.

Giving the parasites power to wield.

Raising higher those who long held power.

Crushing the needy under his soft boot.

His rule seemed sudden to the privileged Few.

The truth is, he always ruled the world.

This time, he chose to come out of the Dark,

To destroy all illusions of justice.

The oppressed refused to suffer his reign.

Finding an iron-will, they struck him down,

That the city on a hill might return.

His disciples had fallen before them,

And the people tried to unite as one.

They had found the will to shed their old fears.

For they had no choice. The city was doomed.

The Orange Prince was not the one at fault,

He simply fed on our base instincts,

Speeding the doom of our city with hate.

Storms shook our very bones. Fury Unchained.

Hunger and thirst stalked us all like fell Beasts.

Yet, hope was not lost. The Fates had Not fled.

With a child's eyes, I saw it all unfold.

Vision and magic they wove together.

Yggdrasil grew to take us to the stars.

An ark as of old, to save what we could.

We lucky few became hope. The future.

In a cacophony of light and chrome,

We left our dead home on an unknown path.

Stars our destination. Twin stars. Siblings.

I, a child gripped my grandparent's hands tight.

As we entered the deep night, they looked down.

Warming me with love, placing me abed.

My soul drifted into sleep's gentle grasp.

I do not know how long I slept and dreamed,

Yet, I awoke with a terrible start.

Screams of the dying. Echoing madness.

Their cries for help shaking my tiny bed.

Burning hair filled my nose, choking my
Voice.

Drenched in fear I faced a swirling
darkness.

My being shook. My throat ached. I was
Lost.

Surrounded by a mad bloody tumult,

I desperately cried for my grandparents.

Violent, twisted wreckage surrounded me.

In the flickering light of the crimson
Flames,

Shadowy forms shifted all about me.

I saw my grandparent's dear friends.
Bloody. Mad.

Fury filled their eyes. Ichor stained their
Hands.

Awakened like me, yet so unlike me.

In my terror I crawled away from hell,

Hunting the deep shadows for my
Grandma.

Hiding in a hole, trembling with such
Fright.

Compassion, hope had died. Killed by
Madness.

Dreams of the future gone. Sweet mercy, gone…

My mind sat on the precipice. Despair!

My very soul consumed. Horror held me.

What had we become in the endless void?

Our forebears would have wept on seeing us.

At that moment, I thought all had been lost.

Then I heard something. Words fail to describe.

A song. A song of love. Hope. Redemption.

At first a murmur, slowly building up,

It wrapped me in comfort, for They had come.

Their song filled up the space. It pushed hate
        Out.

Their song washed over us. Held us. We sang!

Voices unbidden became a choir.

Heavenly lights consumed us. Blinded us.

Washing away the pain and the madness.

The deadly dance of violence stumbled.

The air grew thick. Stillness filled up our hearts.

Then slowly, ever so slowly it stopped.

Only peace remained. Only calm and
Warmth.

Our vision cleared and the ruin was gone.

No more was there shattered glass all
About.

The fire twisted black metal disappeared.

The mangled bodies in peaceful repose.

We no longer sat amongst destruction.

They had brought us to the
Amphitheater.

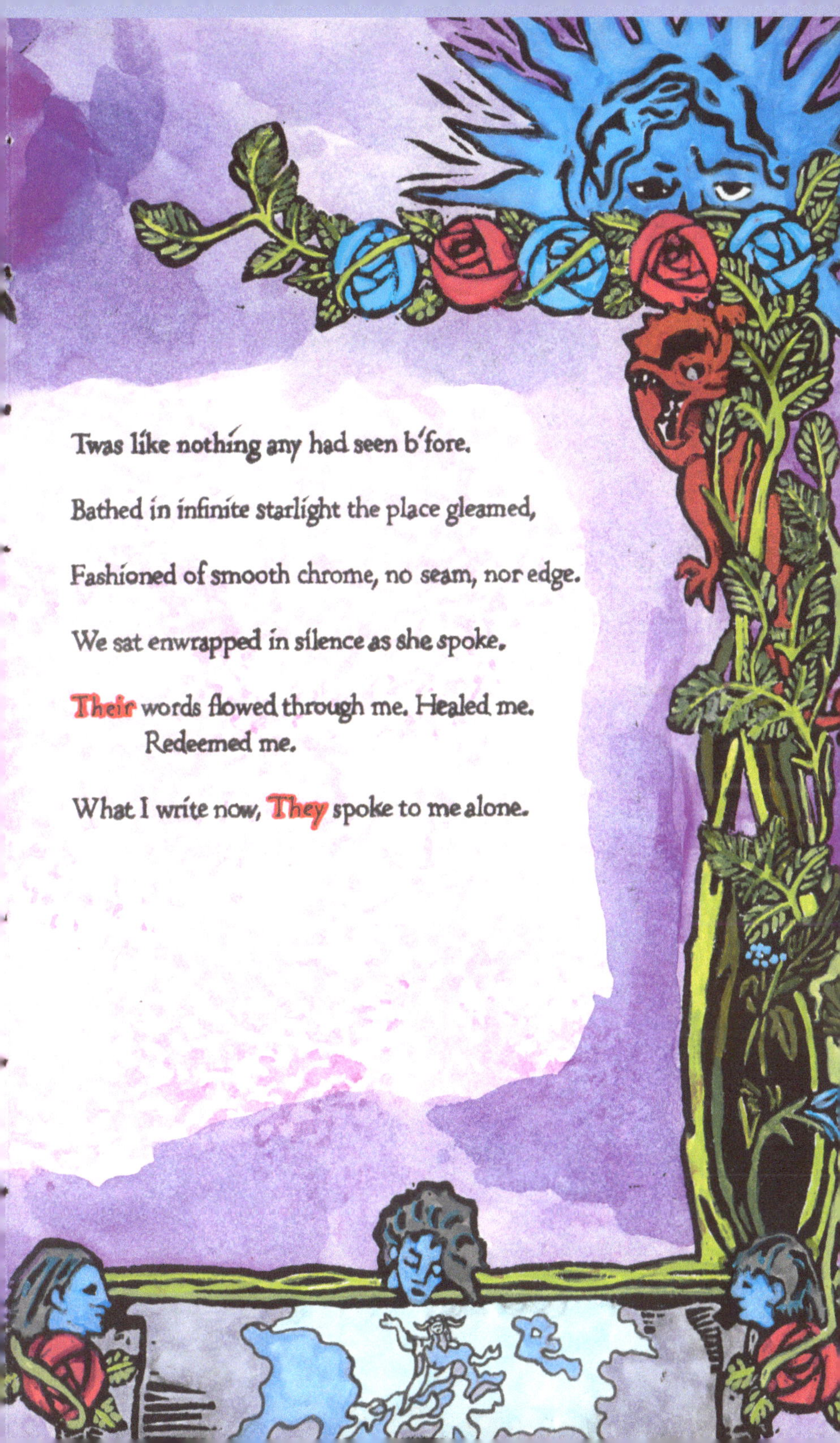

'Twas like nothing any had seen b'fore.

Bathed in infinite starlight the place gleamed,

Fashioned of smooth chrome, no seam, nor edge.

We sat enwrapped in silence as she spoke.

Their words flowed through me. Healed me.
Redeemed me.

What I write now, They spoke to me alone.

My poor child, be at peace and fill thy heart.

Thou hast suffered great pain. Body and soul.

We are here to salve thy wounds. Mend thy hope.

Some hath shed blood and some hath had blood shed.

But, all hath suffered. All are in deep pain.

Let our song embrace thee with my vast love.

Let us shelter thee from the Orange Prince.

Let us expose the Architect of Woe.

With base cunning and sly words he brought death.

He corrupted a few breaking their wills.

They hath all fled from the light of my love,

Into the void they lick their wounds. Take heart!

Let all look to the care of those asleep.

Blissful is their slumber. Peaceful. Unharmed.

Let all repair the dream that was. That is.

That forever shall be. Let all rebuild.

Let a Garden grow over this sorrow.

<br>

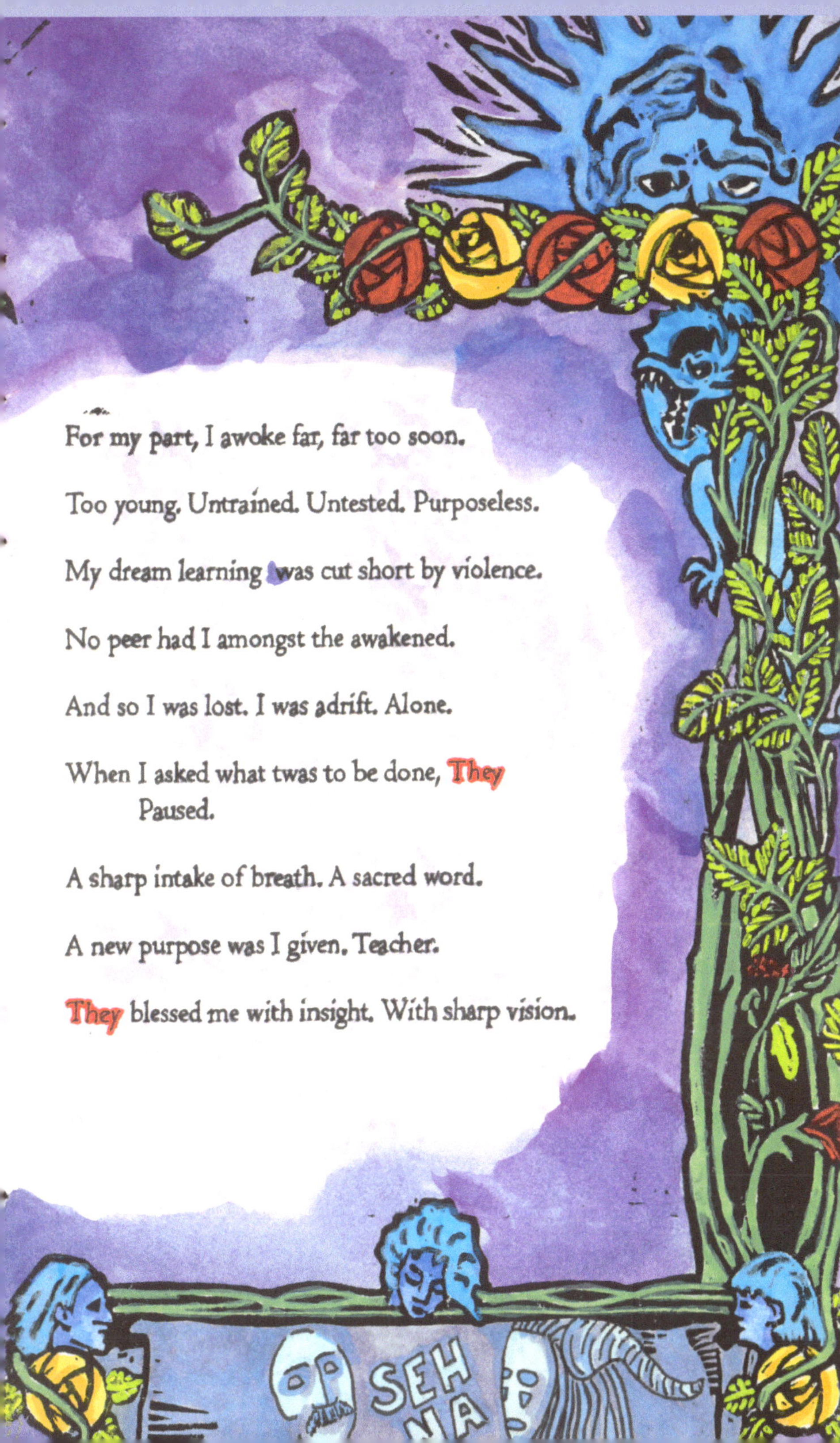

For my part, I awoke far, far too soon.

Too young. Untrained. Untested. Purposeless.

My dream learning was cut short by violence.

No peer had I amongst the awakened.

And so I was lost. I was adrift. Alone.

When I asked what twas to be done, They
    Paused.

A sharp intake of breath. A sacred word.

A new purpose was I given. Teacher.

They blessed me with insight. With sharp vision.

All things under Yggdrasil did I see.

This was the time of finding my purpose.

I learned to see clearly. To come to know.

I learned to teach the wisdom I had
        Found,

Into my care was given the young minds.

Hearts open and willing. Eyes shining
        Bright,

I was not ready for my charge. The weight.

Still, I dove eagerly into my role,

Cloaking myself in the joy of teaching.

So enwrapped, I almost missed it. Almost.

Something had started. A note caught my ear.

Discordant. Divergent, dissonant note.

A familiar sound. Raw. Unsavory.

Black malice creeping back into our song.

Young and foolish, I took no swift action.

I chose to wait and watch. To be patient.

I had time in an endless, vast supply.

But time, tis an ocean, Uncaring. Aloof.

We, immortals, don't count time by
Heartbeats.

We count by the life and death of the
Stars.

We forgot urgency. Grew complacent.

The corrupted had returned in disguise.

These Horrors had slipped into the
Garden,

Subtly with malice in their black hearts.

For many years they did plot corruption,

Seeking to please their uncaring master.

On each of us they tested our limits.

Pushing, pulling, cajoling, haranguing,

With their base cunning they attacked our home,

Tainted what should be pure and protected.

Fortunately we were not defenseless.

The Garden was at peace but prepared for war.

Twas defended by seven guardians.

We guided and protected the rest.

We were meant to be the rocks they crashed on.

If only we'd worked as one from the start.

Instead we sought our own path. Our own way.

Dshef the Walker traversed the world.

On bare feet. Searching. Seeking truth.
Answers.

Endlessly he sought to know perfection.

No destination did he have in mind.

His journey was, is the destination.

Charity he did give to those he met.

Nothing he held, would he not give freely

Where there was a need, Dshef would be
Found.

We measured ourselves by his example.

Swit the Blue swam the rivers, lakes and seas.

Smiling and joyful. Deep she dove unbound.

Endlessly she danced, mirthful and playful.

Living moment-to-moment. In the now.

Laughter she did give to those in most need.

Capricious. Wrathful. She was as water.

She crashed. She flowed. No gloom could forbear
        Her.

She was the dancing laughter of our hearts.

Using the Hand gave form to all his
Dreams.

Endlessly he found purpose with his
Hands,

Be it metal or wood. Clay. Flesh or stone.

He saw the soul of the material.

He found purpose in the work he finished.

The gift of craft he gave to all he met.

No idleness could last under his gaze.

He was the driving force to continue.

**Smok the Red** nurtured all living creatures.

Plants. Animals. Life filled her with wonder.

She comforted all life from birth unto death.

Tree or mouse. Man or monster. She found awe.

Astonishment she shared with all who met her.

Caretaker of life. Mourner of the dead.

The endless cycle held no mystery.

She held infinite love of the vast world.

**Mrok the Wyld** ran where others feared
To tread.

Unrelenting. Tireless. Pitiless.

Endlessly she sought new moments
To face.

Testing friends. Foes. Strangers. She
Craved the thrill.

Be it cresting a mountain in winter,

Be it hunting a great beast in summer,

She sought challenges none could face but
Her.

Adventure she brought to all those
She met.

No timidity could hide from her eyes.

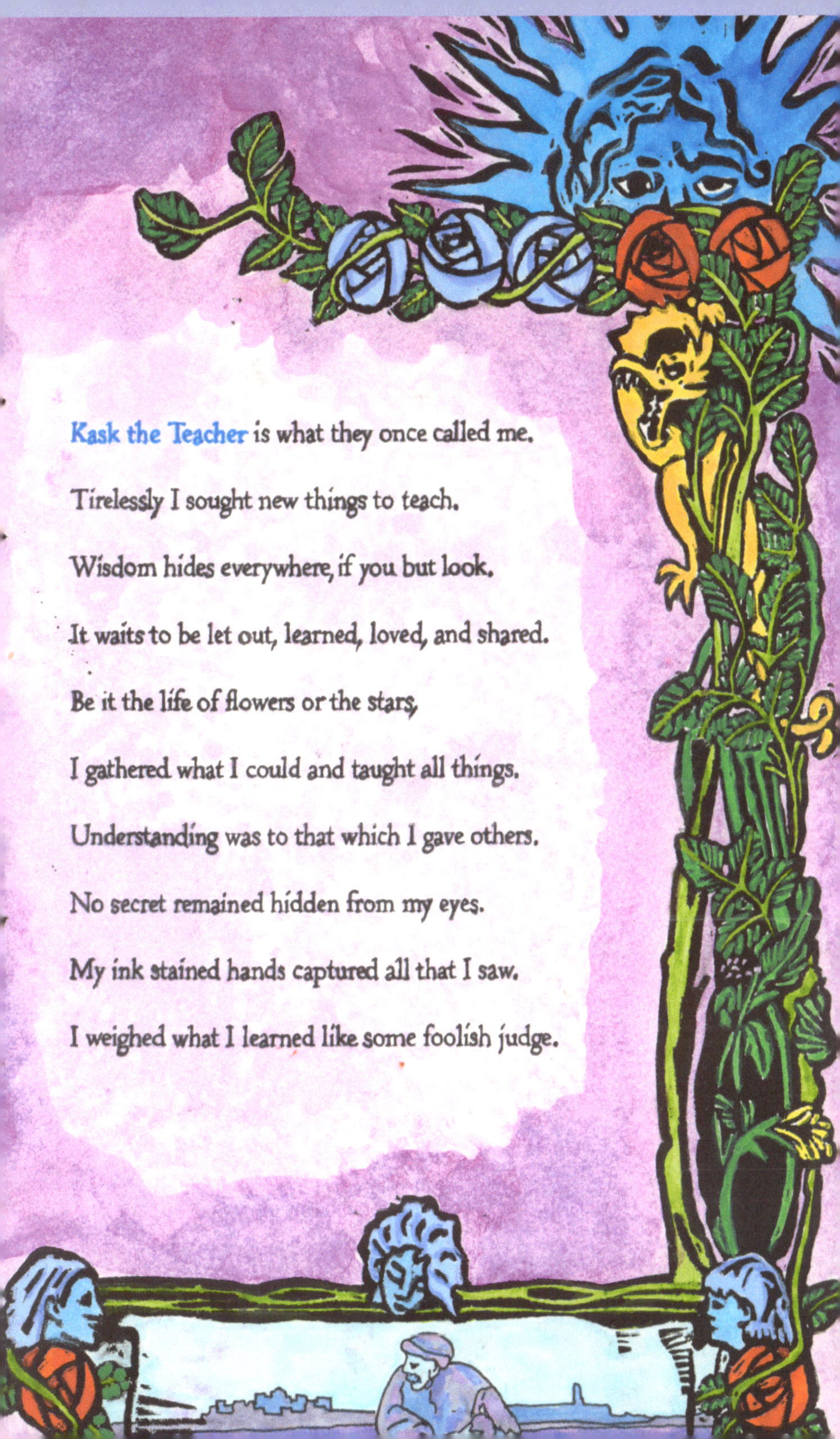

Kask the Teacher is what they once called me.

Tirelessly I sought new things to teach.

Wisdom hides everywhere, if you but look.

It waits to be let out, learned, loved, and shared.

Be it the life of flowers or the stars,

I gathered what I could and taught all things.

Understanding was to that which I gave others.

No secret remained hidden from my eyes.

My ink stained hands captured all that I saw.

I weighed what I learned like some foolish judge.

Goliat the Guardian watched us all.

Purposefully he strode the borderlands.

Sharp was his eye. Quick was his arm
Striking.

Standing vigil. Gazing into the darkness.

Unflinching, the darkness returned his
Gaze.

At the edge of the world he sacrificed.

Gave everything. Asking for nothing.

No evil was he unprepared to face.

Stout heart. Watchful eyes. Steadfast love.
Hero.

He was the standard that measured us all.

We were wardens, but flawed and broken.

Despite our vast age, wisdom, and powers,

Our hubris would be the Garden's sunset.

Our grave mistake haunts fair Yggdrasil
Still.

We feared the Orange Prince's intricate
Web.

We saw a clever foe where there was none.

Blunders became stratagems in our minds.

The Horrors had fooled us? No, We
Fooled ourselves.

Giving no thought to the danger within,

We had let the thief in the door
Unwatched.

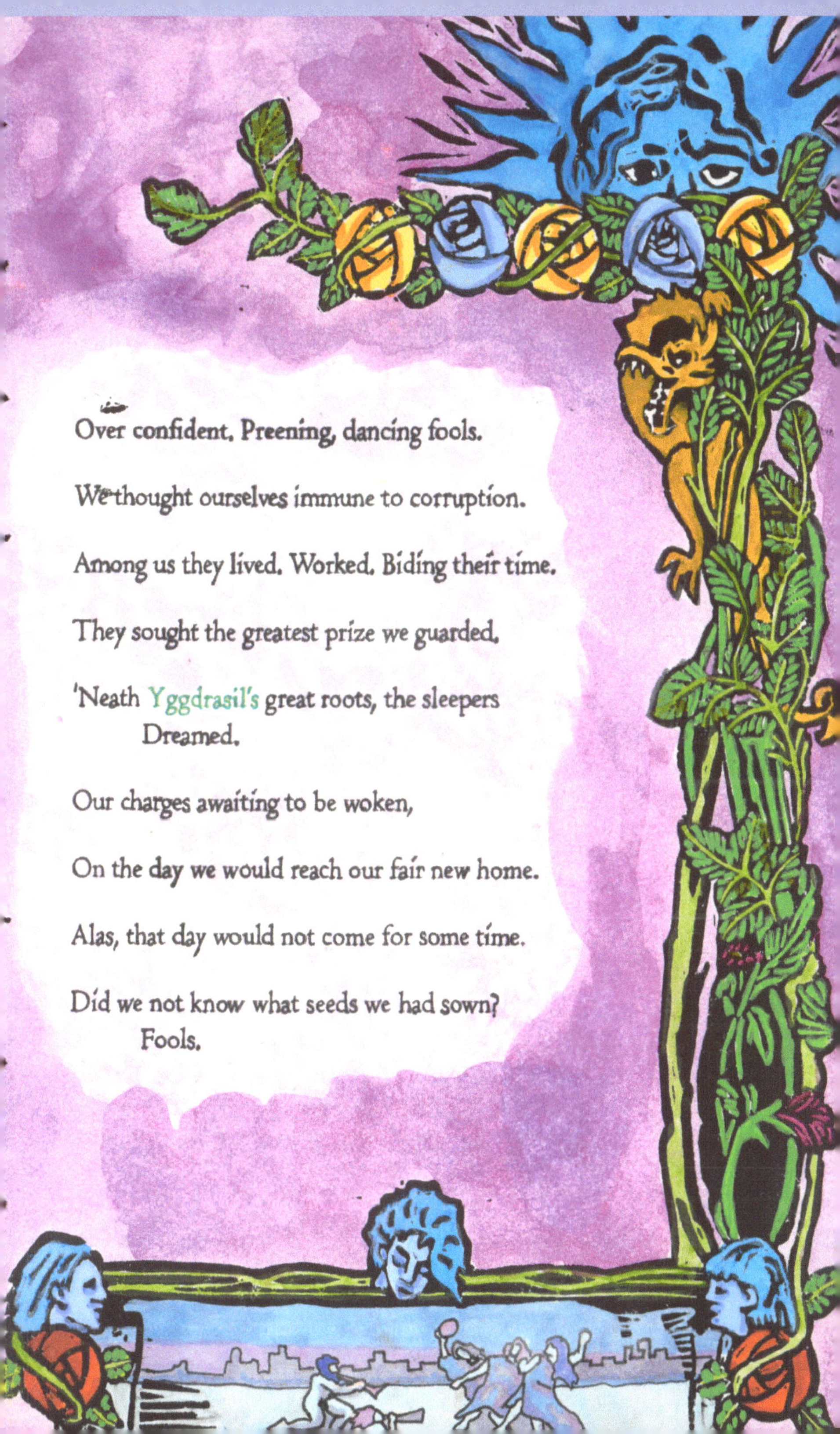

Over confident. Preening, dancing fools.

We thought ourselves immune to corruption.

Among us they lived. Worked. Biding their time.

They sought the greatest prize we guarded.

'Neath Yggdrasil's great roots, the sleepers
      Dreamed.

Our charges awaiting to be woken,

On the day we would reach our fair new home.

Alas, that day would not come for some time.

Did we not know what seeds we had sown?
      Fools.

I cannot blame our loathsome nemesis.

His machinations for our fall could not,

Would not, did not succeed without our
Help.

An evil heart he possesses, tis true.

Yet, stupidity describes him the best.

When mistaken for cunning he blossoms.

When his blundering is exposed, he fails.

And so, in this full flowering, we failed.

So, for a time beyond counting we flew,

Blissful in our ignorance of this truth.

Traveling the stars, onward to our home.

We traversed infinite space together.

Our destination, a new beginning.

A new home bathed in the light of twin suns.

The distant hope of our long dead forebears.

Before us was a limitless future.

A future first found in the cry of babes.

A thousand, thousand years or more had passed.

The joy of babies had been denied us.

The soft sound of love had been forgotten.

We did not expect new joy to be born.

Thus, we were surprised when Gadon
     Showed signs.

Quiet, introspective, slow to action,

Decisive when her course was set. Honest.

Admired. Lovely, curious Gadon.

She was my favorite student. Brilliant.

No father's name ever did pass her lips.

I did not care to learn that mystery.

Beli was first born. Bathed in light.
     Adored.

Under the light of four glorious stars.

She joined our journey, beloved from the
     Start.

Good fortune was the watchword. Majesty.

A queen had been given to us that day.

And yet, she would not be our only gift.

Loud Lut. Brash. Bold. Twitching. Quick to
        Action.

Always rushing when she should be slowing.

Moving. Arguing. Living a full life.

No father's name ever did pass her lips.

I did not care to learn that mystery.

Wagir was second born. Bathed in the light.

He joined our journey, beloved from the start.

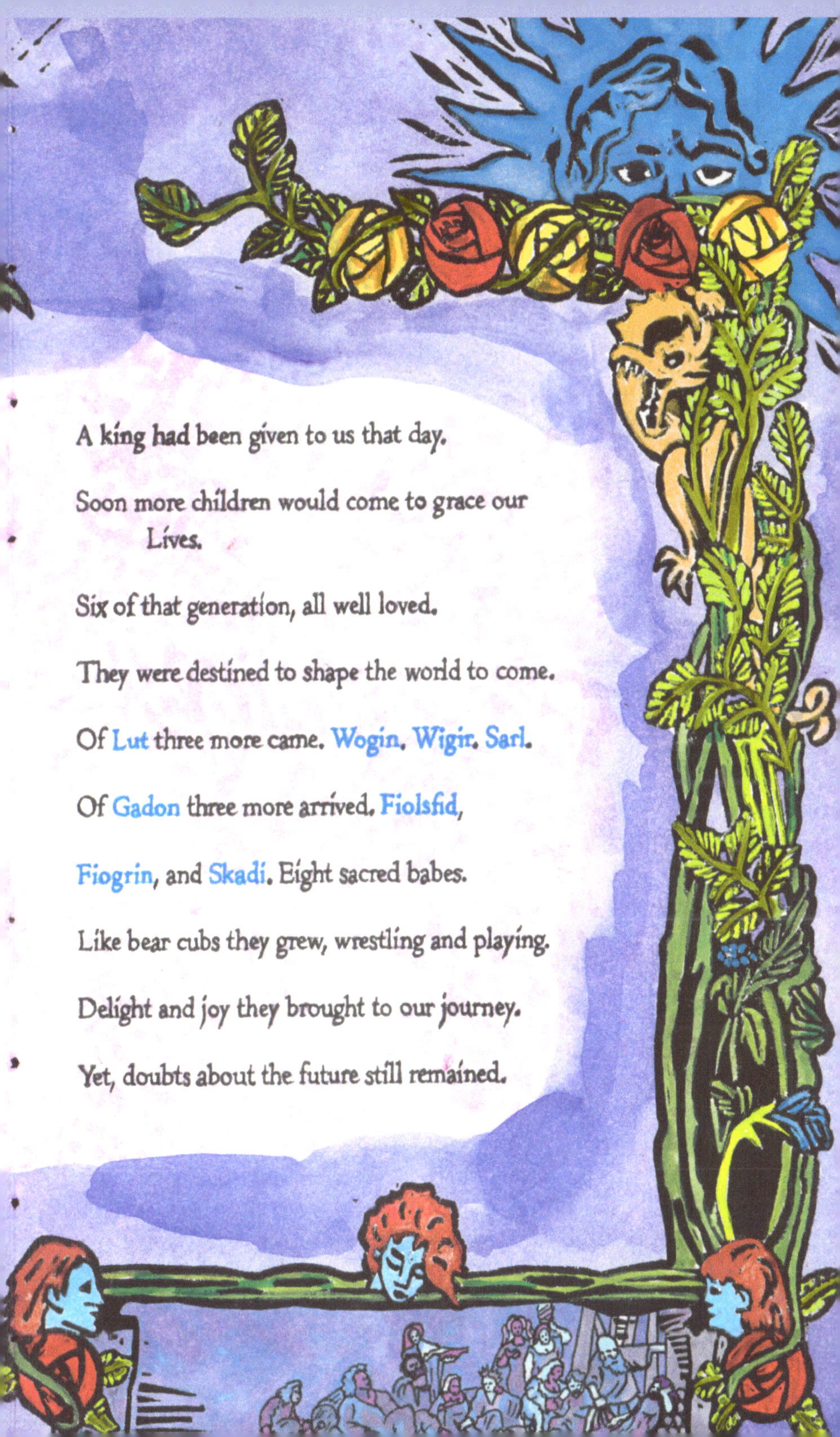

A king had been given to us that day.

Soon more children would come to grace our
        Lives.

Six of that generation, all well loved.

They were destined to shape the world to come.

Of Lut three more came. Wogin, Wigir, Sarl.

Of Gadon three more arrived, Fiolsfid,

Fiogrin, and Skadi. Eight sacred babes.

Like bear cubs they grew, wrestling and playing.

Delight and joy they brought to our journey.

Yet, doubts about the future still remained.

Fear of the unknown joined us. Stained
Our hearts.

An end had come. Foresight was lost to
Us.

We did not see the change in Goliat.

In these births he saw something we did
Not.

He began to ask surprising questions.

Signs that he had changed. Signs we were
Blind to.

He was always the very best of us.

Sacrificing joy for duty and death.

Facing the many threats on our journey.

Threats that came from within and from
Without.

He was our glorious champion. Feared.

Beloved. Trusted. Power filled him fully.

He wrestled with the dread Wurm
of Muspelheem,

Making his armor of its shining scales.

He held back the White hordes of
Rapeto,

From their death songs he crafted
Symphonies.

He slew dread Sothis of Sagarmatda.

With his blood he anointed Sarl of Lut.

We heaped endless glory on our brother.

Weak payment for a life well sacrificed.

For him no boon was ever unanswered.

My family all blame the Orange Prince.

They blame Horrors and the Chittering Dark,

For what was to come. For the darkness and
      Strife.

Our issue lay the blame on my brother.

In him they saw betrayal. Lust and wrath.

Only Sarl and I know the truth of things.

Alas he is now dead and gone. And I…

I will not speak of such sorrow. Such shame.

His transformation seemed shocking.
    Sudden.

Beautiful. Violent. Painful and sorrowed.

War returned to the world once more.
    Blood flowed.

The Garden burned. Horrors rejoiced
    And laughed.

In our ears the voice of a dead tyrant.

Loss became the blanket 'neath which we
    Slept.

Delusion became the wine that we drank.

Betrayal flavored the food which we ate.

Death stalked us like a starving beast.
    Searching.

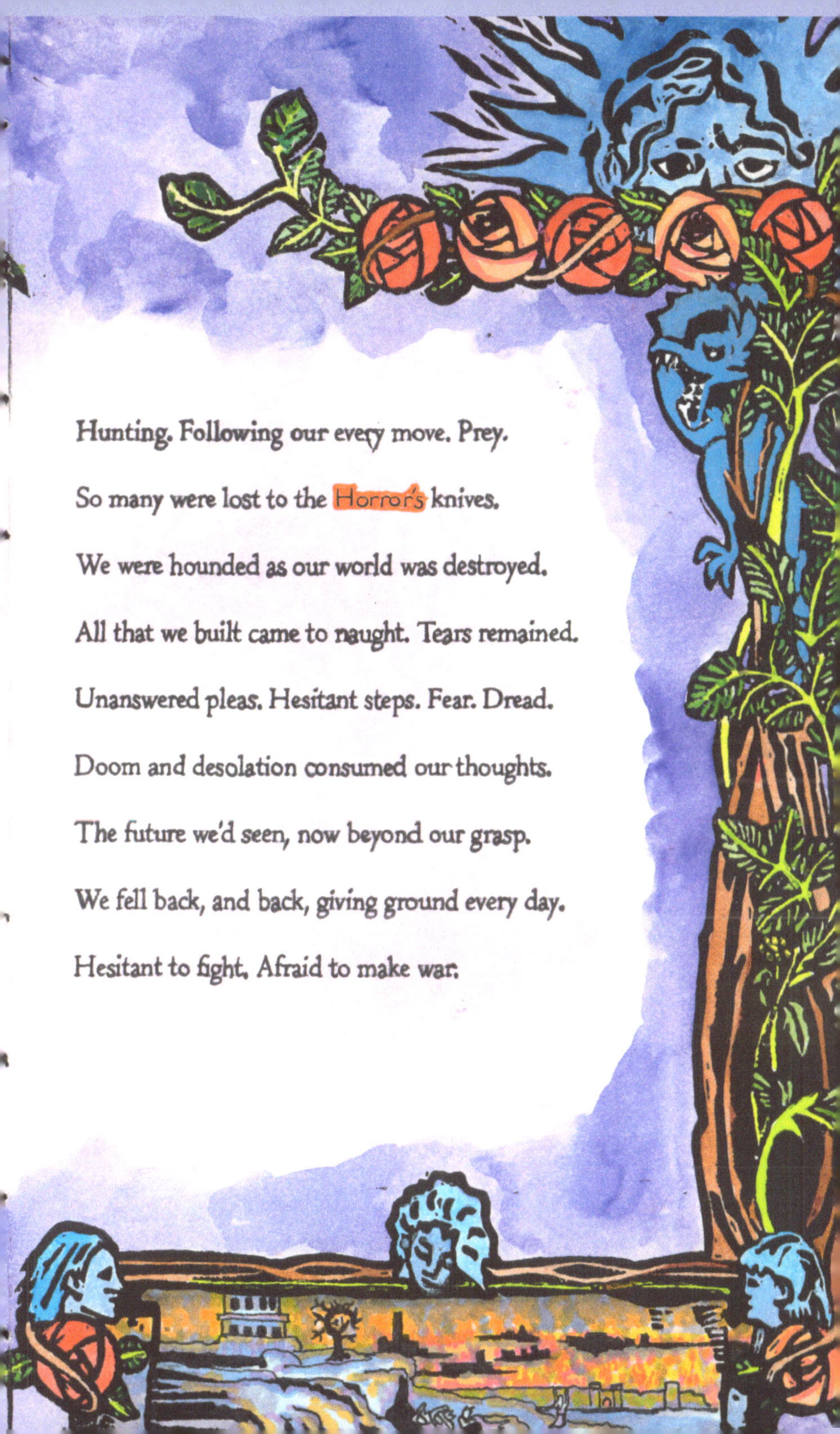

Hunting. Following our every move. Prey.

So many were lost to the Horror's knives.

We were hounded as our world was destroyed.

All that we built came to naught. Tears remained.

Unanswered pleas. Hesitant steps. Fear. Dread.

Doom and desolation consumed our thoughts.

The future we'd seen, now beyond our grasp.

We fell back, and back, giving ground every day.

Hesitant to fight. Afraid to make war.

Til wise Dshef drew a line in the sand.

I will not sacrifice all that we built.

We've given up far too much already.

Too many retreats. No more! Not again!

Here! We draw the line! Here we make our stand!

This far! No further! Here they break on us!

And in that moment our spines grew
    Solid.

And with that our anger became weapons.

And with that we rekindled our lost hope.

Names, there has always been power in them.

The giving. The taking. The renaming.

It traps the shapeless to a single form.

It binds it. Makes the unknowable known.

And so Dshef bid me bring forth my book.

Thus did Dshef give the nameless their names.

Each Horror he bound to a sole purpose.

All save the greatest, whom he bound with two.

And so I wrote. Day and night. Page by page.

The Book of the Five Hundred and One Names.

Even named, they were too strong. Too
Much.

Endlessly they crashed over us like waves,

Pulling us into the eternal dark.

As sand on the beach. Beaten and broken.

And so we gathered to create once more.

Thus Dshef drew from each of us our
Strength.

Into Osing's care he gave over wrath.

And so from this clay, by starlit hands
Shaped,

They of green-gold fire. The Alfar woke.

ALFAR

A people forged to face the unseen host.

Nimble and quick. Made to be relentless.

In dreams they moved. From shadows did
    They strike.

They gave the Horrors pause. Angered
    Their lord.

And yet, this would not give us victory,

For war and death were not Goliat's goal.

The hope of the future lay in slumber,

The true target of dread Goliat's ire.

And so we gathered to create once more.

Thus Dshef drew from each of us our
    Strength.

ADREENIK

Into Osing's care he gave over love.

And so from this clay, by starlit hands he
Shaped.

Fur and claws they were. The Adreenik
Woke.

A people slow to rage, but fierce when
Raised.

Gentle giants. Made to protect all things.

They awakened the spirits of the world,

Setting them against the corrupt Horrors.

Long we fought and long Yggdrasil
Traveled.

Long we had walked the road in the
Starlight.

Our destination, so far. So distant.

Thus, all were surprised when our movement
     Stopped.

Enemies and friends froze to gaze upward.

First there was a red light reflecting our rage.

Then there was a blue light reflecting our woe.

Not one, but two suns bathed us in glory.

No longer would we live by dim starlight.

Twould once again be bright day and dark night.

Stars our destination. We had arrived.

The promise of our forebears had come true.

The shining city could be made anew.

Everything changed. We rediscovered
Hope.

First we collected our sleeping charges.

One by one we woke the Children of
Dawn.

We sent them to start a new beginning,

Upward, beyond the reach of Goliat,

We bid the Adreenik to be their guides.

Perfect shepherds. Wise, gentle guardians.

They cared for all the flora and fauna.

Be they prey or predator, safe they were.

Our charges safely sent to a new home.

We could now go to red war unhindered.

With an Alfar army, both strong and true,

We turned to face our wayward brother's wrath.

Yggdrasil roiled and shook with our rage.

Betrayal is not a hurt lightly salved.

Revenge we craved. His destruction we sought.

We'd been changed. The Garden was lost to us.

The light of our anger drove out all fear.

Beyond their limits we pushed our dread foes.

The Horrors fled, our brother desperate,

In his time of want, Goliat gave birth.

His hate became life. This life became hate.

Jutun we named them. Giants and monsters.

On and on we fought. Time marked by twin
    Suns.

Tears streaked the soot and blood from our faces.

Fear and dread crept into our hearts once more.

Our desperation became destruction.

We became something new, awful, and sad.

They saw this and stepped in to save us all.

They could not stand our loss. Body and soul.

They whispered in the ear of Kernobog.

The Alfar King learned the deepest
        Secrets.

He led us to the Bridge. To our future.

Kernobog's leadership washed away fear.

We did not falter when Jutun attacked,

Freeing Them to cut out the infection.

The cost. The cost was too high. Far too
        High.

They found him seated upon a grotesque.

A throne fashioned from skulls of his
        Slain kin.

'Neath orange light of flickering madness.

Rage danced in his eyes. Laughter on his
Lips.

And so They wove the mightiest of rites.

They gave Their soul so his evil might be
Bound.

Chained in the depths of our glittering
World,

His hate to simmer til the last day,

When Their strength gives out and all
Hope is lost.

On that day the world will become
Undone,

And my sad brother will rule over ash.

Yet, They forestalled that day so we
Might live,

So that we might find a path from ruin.

We fled across the bridge deep in the Gloom.

At the Hot Gate the Alfar King did stand.

Endlessly they came. His blade a thresher.

Goliat was bound. His Jutun unleashed.

Yet, the king did not falter. Did not fall.

So we left him as he bid us to do.

But he promised us the wisdom They gave.

For a day's rest, he would grant a secret.

A price only the brave return to pray.

Thus, Kernobog, great king, guards the Hot
    Gate.

Thus we trudged onward deep in our sorrow.

Silent. Our heads bowed. Our purpose broken.

Our bright future tarnished forever more.

And yet, Dshef bid us to join our hands,

*Look upward and see the wonders I see.*

We took in the light, let the sounds fill us;

A new home awaited us. Needed us.

Our ascent from darkness was upon us.

A new age dawned. Heiuper was here.